Dear Parents:

Congratulations! Your child is taking the first steps on an exciting journey. The destination? Independent reading!

STEP INTO READING® will help your child get there. The program offers five steps to reading success. Each step includes fun stories and colorful art or photographs. In addition to original fiction and books with favorite characters, there are Step into Reading Non-Fiction Readers, Phonics Readers and Boxed Sets, Sticker Readers, and Comic Readers—a complete literacy program with something to interest every child.

Learning to Read, Step by Step!

Ready to Read   Preschool–Kindergarten
• big type and easy words • rhyme and rhythm • picture clues
For children who know the alphabet and are eager to begin reading.

Reading with Help   Preschool–Grade 1
• basic vocabulary • short sentences • simple stories
For children who recognize familiar words and sound out new words with help.

Reading on Your Own   Grades 1–3
• engaging characters • easy-to-follow plots • popular topics
For children who are ready to read on their own.

Reading Paragraphs   Grades 2–3
• challenging vocabulary • short paragraphs • exciting stories
For newly independent readers who read simple sentences with confidence.

Ready for Chapters   Grades 2–4
• chapters • longer paragraphs • full-color art
For children who want to take the plunge into chapter books but still like colorful pictures.

STEP INTO READING® is designed to give every child a successful reading experience. The grade levels are only guides; children will progress through the steps at their own speed, developing confidence in their reading. The F&P Text Level on the back cover serves as another tool to help you choose the right book for your child.

Remember, a lifetime love of reading starts with a single step!

Copyright © 2001 by Penguin Random House LLC

All rights reserved. Published in the United States by Random House Children's Books, a division of Penguin Random House LLC, New York. Originally published in hardcover in the United States by Viking Children's Books, an imprint of Penguin Random House LLC, New York, in 2001.

Step into Reading, Random House, and the Random House colophon are registered trademarks of Penguin Random House LLC.

Visit us on the Web!
StepIntoReading.com
rhcbooks.com

Educators and librarians, for a variety of teaching tools, visit us at
RHTeachersLibrarians.com

Library of Congress Cataloging-in-Publication Data is available upon request.
ISBN 978-0-593-43252-5 (trade) — ISBN 978-0-593-43253-2 (lib. bdg.)

Printed in the United States of America
10 9 8 7 6 5 4 3 2 1

This book has been officially leveled by using the F&P Text Level Gradient™ Leveling System.

CORDUROY
Makes a Cake

by Alison Inches

illustrated by Allan Eitzen

based on the characters created by Don Freeman

Random House 🏠 New York

"Today is my birthday,"
Lisa said.

"I'm having a party!"

Lisa gave Corduroy a hug.

Then she left for school.

A birthday party? thought

Corduroy.

I will make Lisa a Corduroy Cake!

Corduroy got everything

he needed:

1 cake mix

2 cake pans

2 cans of pink frosting

1 bowl

2 eggs

1 cup of water

And one thing he did not need.

Crash!

A bag of flour.

Corduroy brushed himself off.

Then, *r-r-r-rip!*

He poured the cake mix

into the bowl.

Crack! Plop! Splash!

He added the eggs and water.

Then he turned on the mixer.

WHIRRRR!

The batter hit the walls.

It hit the floor.

It hit Corduroy.

"This is fun!" said Corduroy.

Then he put the batter

into the pans.

But there was not enough batter.

"Oh dear," said Corduroy.

"I need more cake mix."

He looked high and low.

But there was no more cake mix.

Then he saw a box

on the counter.

He opened it.

"A cake!" said Corduroy.

"Now I don't need to make one."

But the cake had nothing on it.

"It needs words," said Corduroy.

He put the pink frosting

into a bag.

"I can write on it," he said.

"But first I need practice."

He took the frosting

to the bathroom.

He wrote on the tub.

He even wrote on the mirror.

"Wow!" said Corduroy.

"Now I am good!"

Then, *Click!*

He heard a key in the door.

"Somebody's coming!"

said Corduroy.

He ran into the sewing

room and hid under a shelf.

Clunk!

A box fell on his head.

Then he heard a voice

in the kitchen.

"What a mess!" cried the voice.

Lisa's mother! thought Corduroy.

He listened to her feet.

Click, click, click.

They walked one way.

Click, click, click.

They walked the other way.

Sweep! Bang! Clank!

The feet ran upstairs

and into the bathroom.

He heard a shout.

The feet ran downstairs.

Corduroy came out from under

the boxes.

He felt terrible.

He had not made a cake for Lisa.

He had just made a mess.

But then Corduroy had an idea.

He picked up a pink button.

Neat!

And a green button.

Cool!

And another!

And another!

Corduroy got to work.

Soon he forgot about the cake
and the mess.

He even forgot he felt terrible
until . . .

Click! Click! Click!

Lisa's mother!

Corduroy hid inside the box.

She picked up the box with
Corduroy and put it on a table.

Corduroy heard things

from inside the box.

He heard the doorbell.

Ding! Dong!

He heard children's voices.

He heard laughter and horns.

Then he heard
a voice say,
"Where's Corduroy?"
It was Lisa.

"Corduroy will turn up,"

said her mother.

"It's time for presents."

"Yes!" cried her friends.

Lisa opened a big present.

"A tea set!" she said.

Lisa opened a little present.

"A necklace!" she said.

Then she picked up the box

with Corduroy.

"This box looks like a cake!"

said Lisa.

She shook the box.

Corduroy went up and down.

She shook it again.

Corduroy went from side to side.

Then Lisa took off the lid

and looked inside.

"Corduroy!" she cried.

Lisa picked Corduroy up.

"I love my Corduroy Cake!"

said Lisa.

Corduroy felt very proud.

Happy birthday, Lisa! he thought.

"Happy birthday!"

said her friends.

Then they shouted,

"Hooray for Lisa!

Hooray for Corduroy!"

And hooray for my Corduroy Cake!

thought Corduroy.